minions PARADISE™

PHIL SAVES THE DAY!

Adapted by Trey King • Illustrated by Ed Miller

Based on the Minions Paradise *video game*

LB kids

016 © Universal Studios Licensing LLC. Despicable Me, Minion Made and all related marks and characters are trademarks and copyrights of Universal Studios. Licensed by Universal Studios LLC. ll Rights Reserved. In accordance with the U.S. Copyright Act of 1976, the scanning, uploading, and electronic sharing of any part of this book without the permission of the publisher is unlawful iracy and theft of the author's intellectual property. If you would like to use material from the book (other than for review purposes), prior written permission must be obtained by contacting the lisher at permissions@hbgusa.com. Thank you for your support of the author's rights. • Little, Brown and Company • Hachette Book Group • 1290 Avenue of the Americas, New York, NY 10104 • Visit us at lb-kids.com • LB kids is an imprint of Little, Brown and Company. The LB kids name and logo are trademarks of Hachette Book Group, Inc. • The publisher is not responsible for websites (or their content) that are not owned by the publisher. • First Edition: May 2016 • ISBN 978-0-316-39296-9 • 10 9 8 7 6 5 4 3 2 1 • CW • minionsparadise.com

Printed in the United States of America

It's been a long time since the Minions had a vacation.

This year, the whole tribe decided on a tropical cruise for their vacation. As they sail the seven seas, there are all kinds of fun activities—and things to eat. The buffet is filled with recipes featuring the Minions' favorite foods: banana splits, banana pudding, banana bread, banana cake… they have it all!

The Minions each have something to share.

Charlie is making balloon animals!

Barry makes his famous burritos.

Amazing chef Ken makes
a delicious banana cake!

And then there's Phil...

Phil has a habit of messing things up. While hula dancing, Phil accidentally knocks over Ken's delicious cake, ruining it for his buddies.

BOINK!

Everyone walks away upset at Phil.
No one likes dirty floor cake. Poor Phil.

Phil tries to think of a way to make
it up to the other Minions.

He makes balloon animals—
but they keep popping!

He makes burritos—
but they're way too spicy!

He even tries to make a cake—
but he burns it beyond recognition.

Phil decides some harmless sunbathing might be a good way to spend the rest of his day.

But a well-oiled Minion makes things a little slippery....Phil better hold on to something. Oops! Too late!

Phil is as slippery as a bar of soap! As he slides
all over the ship, he makes a real mess of things.

When he hits the captain's wheel, Phil knocks the ship off course!
Hold on, everybody!

The ship crashes into a large rock, causing water to start pouring in.

Ahhhh!

Phil flies off the ship and skips across the water like a stone. He lands on a deserted island. Phil's really done it this time!

Uh-oh! The ship is sinking, and all the Minions are making a swim for it. They do *not* look happy.

What is Phil going to do?!

Phil has ruined the other Minions' vacation.
Boy, are they mad! He'd better hurry!

A coconut falls from above and hits
Phil in the head. This gives him an idea!

BOINK!

Phil makes a tiki lounge! He also makes welcome baskets for everyone. And he makes lots of smoothies!

Everyone gets a banana drink from the smoothie bar! Suddenly, being trapped on a deserted island doesn't seem so bad. Good job, Phil!

Now the whole tribe is on an island and having the time of their lives. There are games for everyone and a pool with water slides. But the best part of all…is the amazing food! Who wants more banana smoothies?

So perhaps Phil *doesn't* ruin everything—
he makes it better! He's turned a disaster into a party!
Well done, Phil!